T0195851

Following Jesus as a Lady Disciple

To order additional copies of this book, contact:
Xlibris
844-714-8691
www.Xlibris.com
Orders@Xlibris.com

ISBN: Softcover   979-8-3694-0449-2
        EBook   979-8-3694-0450-8

Print information available on the last page

Rev. date: 08/03/2023

Following Jesus as a Lady Disciple

by

Ruth Brown

Dedication

This book is dedicated to my Savior Jesus Christ.

To all my children, grandchildren and great grand children.

My adopted children that stuck by me when my youngest son found dead in a Super 8 motel room in Columbus in 2014

My Pastor Deborah Austin Sanders who helped me more that she will ever know.

Thank you

This is a story of Jesus and his many followers, but I will be Priscilla the lady disciple who follows Christ after his walk to his cousin John the Baptist to be baptized.

I will tell what I saw during the 3 years that He was walking the earth. To prepare people He chooses to be His disciples and the events that follow leading up to His death on the cross.

Watching all that was involved with Him and how they may have felt during the times when the events of His life happened.

This is a story not quoted but God inspired some things to help get close to Jesus, and helping to understand His purpose.

We are to start with Jesus walking up to his cousin John the Baptist to be baptized.

This is exactly what is expected of Jesus because in the teachings it was written before he was born. Jesus being the son of God, whatever was told back in the day was on paper somewhere, making all that Jesus did a history.

Jesus was being baptized a dove came down towards him and you hear a voice from heaven say this is my son and I am extremely proud of him. Whoever was paying attention knew he was not a person from anyone around him because they were baptized and no doves and voices from heaven.

Jesus then had to be in the desert of wilderness to prepare for his life's journey. This was also predicted. Forty days in prayer and fasting. No food or water. The devil was trying to make his day bad by promising him stuff that he had no power over. Knowing that he was a liar. Jesus was a good-natured and kind but He knew what He had to do and no one could change His mind.

Jesus was on His 30th day and the devil was back promising to turn rocks into bread. Jesus said to him. Devil begone. He had to leave because he cannot stay where he is not wanted. Jesus had to go and collect men to follow him and make them fishers of men.

He had to have people to teach what he was already taught. He learned a lot from attending Temple School.

A few men sought Him out that had been following John the Baptist. They that followed John the Baptist will now follow Jesus. When they watched Jesus, they learned how He felt about people. Jesus wanted 12 people to be constant followers of him. Since I am following Jesus these will be actual events. Nothing is quoted but events in no particular order.

These are events that had happened as we walk with Jesus during His 3 years on earth as a 30 year old man. Jesus starts by teaching His disciples some of the rules for life like the 10 commandments, and how to pray.

Jesus also mentions to them they should always pray to the Father in heaven as well as when helping others.

Jesus says, when praying the Lord's prayer it covers a multitude of things and it is a basic prayer that gets God's attention every time. Jesus teaches also that healing a body of anyone is part of God's direction.

First of all you have to see what ails a man or a woman. Then you assess the problem and hand the situation over the Father.

Examples are:

A man comes to Jesus as a lepard. This means he has a disease no one acknowledges or wants with boils that seep and sores all over his body and he smells really bad. Jesus prays over the man and tells him to go deep himself 7 times in the river. This is healing process. Then the man does as Jesus says and goes to the river and each time he goes under water and out, his skin heals so by the 7th time he is completely healed.

I finished watching this healing, I was hungry so I went to my cousin's house. Jesus was going the same way but He was on route to go and have dinner with a tax collector. I went to eat with my cousin Sarah and to ask her to come along with me on my journey to follow Jesus. She said ok.

She wants to follow us so she would be with me and I would be not alone in this journey. The rule is not to be on a journey by yourself. Especially a woman. Even men do not journey by themselves.

Sarah agreed to come with me. Sometimes Jesus likes to be a far away just send up prayers. So when following him it's a good idea to have someone with you that you can communicate with because men folk may have other ideas when seeing a woman alone.

We are on our way to the tax collectors house where Jesus is having dinner. There are also some men from the temple following behind Jesus as well. For some odd reason they are keeping an eye on him, because everywhere He goes he draws crowds of people.

They are asking questions to try and find out why so many people and if He is a threat to them. I Priscilla and Sarah are walking towards the boat where Jesus is going to give His next teaching for all of us. Jesus is in the boat next to a bunch of rocks where His disciples will be seated and we are in hearing distance along the shore. Jesus's voice is so crisp and clear. Every word from His mouth we can understand.

Blessed are the meek. They shall inherit the earth. He says- to explain meek and inherit. To understand the problems of people. To inherit to be able to put into place what everyone may need. Give a helping hand. It is about making sure your fellow man is comfortable. Jesus gave an hour of teaching on these laws and then Jesus said, we must treat our fellow men just as if we were teaching ourselves. Love your neighbor as yourself. Do not do bad things to your neighbor that you would do to you. Keep God above everything. God is our Father and He should be considered in everything that we do. Do not do things in haste.

Consider God when doing anything. That way you keep Him first and keep things in order. Jesus was finished with His teaching for now. He was going to have prayer time by Himself on a hill nearby. Sarah and me, we are going to find some apples to eat. We found some pretty yellow apples and they tasted good. Jesus returned and asked some of His disciples to pick out a few people to pray with them. Jesus gathered us together and prayed over us all. This is to give us power from the Father above. Putting God first.

Remember always pray. Always group yourselves together to be able to have that boost only God can give. This is God's work. One disciple says, my Lord, what do I do when someone wants a child healed and the child is not with the person? Jesus replies pray and ask the name. Then tell them by the time you get to the child because of your faith the child will be healed. God is watching.

Sarah says to me. Why do you follow this man? I have never heard of him or read anything about him. Priscilla says, Sarah you have not read any of the old teachings from the prophets before now? No Sarah says, my house does not go to the temple or gather to pray like these people or even you. Priscilla asks, Do you want to learn? Your heart and your being have to yearn for to learn to love.

Jesus Christ is about love and understand that His purpose is to bring all hearts to be His. To love God the Father with all you are. Pray and God will guide you. You have to want to love the Lord. Sarah says. OK. Can you help me. Yes I will help you.

First of all you need to learn how to pray. Now Jesus gave a prayer to His disciples. It is called the Lord's prayer. Before I teach you. You have to open your heart.

There is a God that has power to give you the want to. He is called the Father. He is the creator of all living beings and He created both of us. I have been studying Christ before He was born by John the Baptist what He is all about. When studying the old teachings predict both John the Baptist and Jesus Christ being born through their mothers who are cousins. So they are cousins.

Let us pray a prayer from the heart.

Father in heaven open our hearts and minds to serve you. To give of ourselves the want to learn of you and your son Jesus Christ. To be able to love ourselves as well as others and to understand the purpose of our lives.

Thank you for your love to keep us surrounded and grounded.

Sarah says. Thank you Priscilla I feel a bit uneasy. I never prayed and it is making me feel different. Priscilla says, I think that is God the Father working on the inside of you. You will feel more like wanting to pray. Apparently you are sincere in wanting to know God. Otherwise you would not feel anything. Wow Let's get some sleep period Jesus does not stay in one place too long. Sarah there is a lot of things and prayers and old teachings you need to know. The Lord put it on my heart to teach you about some of the prophets, judges and kings back before Jesus was born.

You need to know to understand what our purpose for following Jesus is. What we do know is Jesus is about helping people and always loving people and trying get as many people to love and understand Him. Sarah ask why so much information? Am I going to have to remember everything?

Well you need to remember some basic things but as we live with and around Jesus you will get more of an understanding as God the Father gives us knowledge. We will start your teaching with learning about a man named Samuel who was considered a prophet and a judge. He got commands from God the father and would do as God would ask of him God directed many people.

Samuel learned from the temple priests as a child to hear the voice of God and to obey. Everything you learn will eventually lead to Jesus the Christ. Now Samuel was given a job to do and that was to anoint kings. At this point in his life he anointed the king of Israel, who was Saul. We are not going to discuss Saul but the next king which would be called David.

David was a shepherd but took care of sheep in a pasture and as he took care of these animals he would sing to them and write down what he would sing. He would take care by keeping wild animals away from these sheep so the animals would not harm the sheep. When he wrote songs he left many to be put on scrolls. Samuel came looking for David because God told him to anoint him. Samuel had to find David because he was the youngest of all his brothers. Samuel had stones that changed colors if the person he was seeking did not change the color of the stones, then he had to keep going until this event happened. He went to every one of David's brothers and there was no color change, so Samuel had to ask if there was any other.

David's father said there is one more out in the pasture. David was called. Some will put stones under his chin and they change colors. Samuel anointed him as asked of him by God. Anointed means pouring oil on a person's head.

David's had a song to sing and he made the song known before he became king. The song is the Lord is my Shepherd. I'm teaching this to you to show you this is what we are. Sheep like David's. And our Shepherd is Jesus Christ. See how this fits. This will give you a better idea of why we are God's sheep. If you don't learn nothing else from me you should learn this.

The Lord is my shepherd I shall not want. Sarah says. The Lord is my shepherd I shall not want. The Lord is going to watch me like David watches his sheep. Priscilla says: The Lord's sheep he keeps a watchful eye on and he will provide for whatever you need.

It is also like the birds of the field. God takes care of them and they don't need what we need like food, clothing a place to sleep. We are looked by our God just that way. Jesus is going to his post to teach us something more.

Jesus is saying when coming into a situation, where it is in your face. Like someone needs to walk after being lame all of their lives. Get power from above. A simple prayer is.

Lord this person has been waiting for an answer from you and is asking with a pure heart and wants divine help. It is not by my power the healing comes but from you Lord. Thank the Lord for the healing power. Tell the person to get up your faith has made you whole. Rise and walk. In all that you do and all that you say. God is your guide. Don't ever forget that. You represent the higher power. Nothing you do is of yourself. You are a vessel being used with the power from God. Jesus also says sometimes you need to be aware of things that jump into your mind quickly and you will have to do things fast.

For example a blind person may be right there asking for help being blind from birth. What you should do. Make a mud pack put on persons eyes praying all while you are making this. Put mud on both eyes thanking God for his power and asking person to go wash it off in river. Allowing the person to go is building the person's faith and by the time the person reaches the river soon as the mud is rinsed off the eyes will be healed and the person will be able to see. Jesus offers up another prayer as he closes his teaching event.

Father of all maker of heaven and earth. Thank you for your presence. Love you with our whole hearts. We offer our thanks. Thank you for your gracious power. Amen.

Priscilla says now that our Lord Jesus is finished with his teaching. I have another person from the old teachings I want you to learn about. It's another woman and her name is Deborah. A person that God used because she had an ear to hear what God had to say to her.

The Lord calls ordinary people to do extraordinary things. Deborah was one of these people. She was a judge just like Samuel. She was picked by God to be a mouth piece. She heard what God had to say to her and used what she heard to help the fight an army of men 10 times its size by the commands that the Lord gave her to give to the commander of the Israelites, that was to take over this other army of men.

We have a job to do as disciples of Jesus Christ. We have to pray for our duties. We have to love our fellow men. We have to ask the Lord for power to do these things which are set before us. We have to show kindness and be firm in our beliefs. The Lord is in His holy temple let all the earth keep silence before him. Let us sing to the Lord, let us dance before the Lord. Let us rejoice in His holy name. That He strengthens us in what He wants us to do.

We need His strength and we need to praise the Lord at all times. Pray and Praise. Make a joyful noise before the Lord. To give us strength and to help keep the spirit high so all who is around us can feel the strength that is coming above. It's time to find some food. Let's go get a fish or fruit. There are olive trees over in the field. There are some rocks we can sit on after we pick the ripe olives. Ok. I'm a bit hungry too says Sarah. It will be time for Jesus to teach another lesson. So after we eat we can go and see what Jesus is going to teach us all today. Jesus says my friends you should know a lot of the old teachings from the scrolls because it's part of my heritage. I have spoken about long time ago. In the teachings people resorted to praying to something you can see instead of a God that's not visible but is around.

When our people were moving along from captivity from Egypt. They could not clearly think. That a God is surrounding them. The God that was with them showed that He was there. By being a cloud for them in the daylight and a fire for them at night. They wanted something they themselves could see and touch. So they made a golden calf. They began giving their praise and worship to this golden calf. When their leader was up talking to God to get rules for them to live by. There was a huge mountain and it rumbled as their leader was getting rules and they were giving their praise and worship to a man made gold calf.

The leader returned illuminated from being in the presence of God and it didn't matter to them. The leader made them give up their golden calf. The calf was considered an idol. Something to praise. They wanted a God they could see. Jesus was finished with the teaching about idols.

Priscilla is starting her teaching to Sarah. Priscilla says the other person I want to teach you about is King Hezekiah. God picked this man because he believed in the true and living God. Hezekiah heard from God and would follow God's instructions. Some people actually do the opposite of what God wants. They get into trouble. Hezekiah had to build an underground water. Water supply to reach our warriors without the enemies finding out about how water was getting to our camps. That had to take a lot of patience and know how. God always has the answer to any situation. Priscilla says WOW we have been taught about the invisible God for a long time with John the Baptist. So I do understand Jesus's message. Sarah say I understand it better than before. I would like to understand more. Priscilla I cannot be with you and not understand what Jesus is all about. Well Sarah one really important thing to do to understand Jesus more is to have the want to. Which you seem to have and the other thing you have to do is to be baptized like all that follow Jesus.

When you become baptize you become part of the family of believers and the invisible God helps you when you pray because your spirit is joined with his spirit and you fall in love with God and want to do everything you can to understand the words and actions of Jesus. Jesus Christ was born to bring all to God. He is God's son and He is going to lead you to His Father. It is written on the scrolls He talks about it at temple. We are going to pray until we fall asleep. We will pray that the invisible God hears our prayers and work with us during our sleep so we are prepared to go to the water in the morning. We both have to be ready and I know God loves it when somcone wants full communication with Him. Thank you Lord for the love you have for both of us and meet us in the morning.

Sarah it's time to get a white shawl to put over your shoulders after your baptism. We are going to the nearest river which is the Jordan river. It will be in sight about 280 cubits. I will walk into the water praying God meets me there and I will call you.

Father I have the authority under the leadership of John the Baptist to baptize and I and my cousin need your confirmation now. Thank you for being here. Sarah come into the water. Sarah says I'm nervous. That's OK. God won't let nothing happen to you. You got this far. No reason to turn back now. OK. Cross your arms and hold your nose.

I baptized you Sarah Higgins with power from above and water. God will also baptize you with His Holy Spirit. Water over your head by the Father. Water over your head by the son. Water over your head by the Holy Spirit. Amen.

It is done Sarah you may put on your shawl. Oh Priscilla I'm shaking and crying and I just want to sing and praise God. I feel wonderful. Good, God is pleased says Priscilla.

We have to go for a teaching from Jesus now. It will be soon and we are a bit further out that we are usually are from Him. We can pick some fruit from the Sycamore tree that is on our way and eat as we walk.

Sarah says, I have never had this tasty little fruit. This is a very new experience. Yes well you will experience more than you have ever, because you have been kept in a home and have had no adventures.

This is your time to experiment with different tastes and maybe some challenges you won't be alone. We are coming upon a different river and see Jesus in a boat. He is getting ready to teach. We made good time. There are rocks to sit on and people all around. I'm going to teach on tithing today says Jesus. In the teachings there was a man named Abraham. He was called the Father of many nations and one of God's many followers.

What many don't know is tithing was practice many years ago. Even before Abraham God the Father requests that people that work or sell animals or vegetables to market and receive money or trade for animals must give the best of their crops a portion to the Priests. If you have no crops or you have no cattle or sheep then you would give birds.

You have to give the best sheep or goat you raised. You had to give 10th of whatever kept you going for the year.

The 10th from each family to the Priests keeps the temple in good shape. I earlier mentioned Abraham. He had 12 sons and many sheep. The sons took care of the sheep. Abraham each year had to answer to his priest Melchezadek and give his 10%. Sometimes it was money, sometimes it was a few baby lambs. Sometimes it may have been vegetables.

This rule does not change. Just like paying taxes. We have to give 10% to God through our Priests. You give God first then yourselves and all things will fall into place because you are keeping God first. Jesus was done with his lesson.

Hi Priscilla I'm going to teach you Sarah about another prophet of God his name is Joshua. Joshua is a leader of the Israelites and took over after Moses. Joshua followed the voice of God like all others. There are always wars to overcome or people trying to defend their areas of land. There was to be a battle between Jericho and Joshua's army. The Lord gave Joshua instructions for 7 days. Each day he was to lead a group around this city using God's army. Using horns for 6 those 7 days.

The last day the people of Joshua's army was to use their voices to shout loud. They gave all they had in their voices and the very walls of the city of Jericho fell.

This was a victory for the army of Joshua because of following God's instructions. You can achieve much, even defeating a city. Sarah says WOW God is a mighty force and believing in Him is a good rule to follow. Sarah I just got word that Jesus is asking that we meet Him over beside the bank of the river. He wants to talk to His followers directly.

Jesus says to us I had a very large vision during my sleep. The vision starts out with being in a large room. I share with you here my bread and wine. I ask one of you to go and do what was planned for you to do. I wash each of your feet. While speaking to you individually. I am then taken with a small army of men. I am judged by a few different people. I am accused by a bunch of people to be crucified. I am beaten really bad. Bleeding from some kind of thorn crown. I am made to carry a very heavy cross. I am hung on this cross between two prisoners. I have a conversation with them. I am stabbed in the side with a spear. My mother and brothers are standing at my feet as I hang from this cross. I am praying to my Father that is in heaven. The sky is getting dark and the winds is picking up. I die. I got taken off the cross up to a tomb. There is a cloth put on my face. I am laid in this tomb. The tomb is covered by a huge stone. No man can move. I lay in this tomb for two nights. On the morning of the third day. My Father comes and gets me. We rise together and the tomb is opened. I am no longer there. I come back and see some of you bringing spices to tomb. I tell them to go tell others. I have raised from death to life. I will meet and give instructions. For what you are to do and go tell everyone the good news. Being a vision this is what I will have to go through. This evening I will meet with all of you together in this huge room at the top of building.

We go and the building has a room with a very long table that seats more than a dozen people with a wine jug a plate with a large flat bread and a cup. In the corner is a basin with water and drying towels. Jesus comes in and washes our feet. Sarah and I sit at table as Jesus washes all feet. I say to Sarah from the vision we heard earlier. This is the beginning of the end.

Printed in the United States
by Baker & Taylor Publisher Services